Pup and Hound
Play Copycats

For Allison and Emma, the copycat kids, and always, for Holly — S.H.

For Yvette, a copy cat ... and whisker accountant extraordinaire! — L.H.

 Kids Can Read is a registered trademark of Kids Can Press Ltd.

Text © 2007 Susan Hood
Illustrations © 2007 Linda Hendry

Kids Can Press acknowledges the financial support of the Government of Ontario, through the Ontario Media Development Corporation's Ontario Book Initiative; the Ontario Arts Council; the Canada Council for the Arts; and the Government of Canada, through the BPIDP, for our publishing activity.

Published in Canada by
Kids Can Press Ltd.
29 Birch Avenue
Toronto, ON M4V 1E2

Published in the U.S. by
Kids Can Press Ltd.
2250 Military Road
Tonawanda, NY 14150

www.kidscanpress.com

The artwork in this book was rendered in pencil crayon on a sienna colored pastel paper.
The text is set in Bookman.

Series editor: Tara Walker
Edited by Yvette Ghione
Printed and bound in Singapore

The hardcover edition of this book is smyth sewn casebound.
The paperback edition of this book is limp sewn with a drawn-on cover.

CM 07 0 9 8 7 6 5 4 3 2 1
CM PA 07 0 9 8 7 6 5 4 3 2 1

Library and Archives Canada Cataloguing in Publication

Hood, Susan
      Pup and hound play copycats / written by Susan Hood;
illustrated by Linda Hendry.

(Kids Can read)
ISBN 978-1-55453-144-8 (bound)
ISBN 978-1-55453-145-5 (pbk.)

1. Dogs—Juvenile fiction. I. Hendry, Linda II. Title.
III. Series: Kids Can read (Toronto, Ont.)

PZ7.H758Puppl 2007   j813'.54   C2007-901119-5

Kids Can Press is a *corus*™ Entertainment company

Pup and Hound Play Copycats

Written by Susan Hood

Illustrated by Linda Hendry

Kids Can Press

What was that?

An old leather shoe!

Pup pulled it away.

He wanted it, too.

So Hound chased the ducks
quacking their song.

Pup dropped the shoe,

then tagged along.

Hound stopped to visit

the pigs eating slops.

Pup pushed in, too,

smacking his chops.

Hound needed a nap —

a short getaway.

But that tagalong pup

wanted to play.

Hound hid by a tree.

Pup did, too.

Hound hid in a bush.

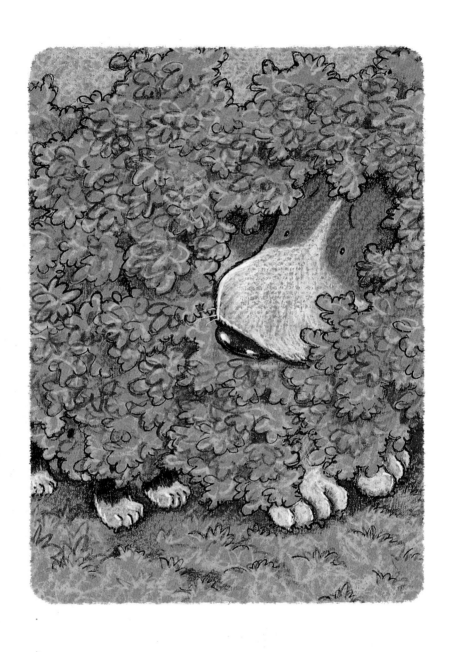

Pup did, too.

Hound went through the gate.

"Woof!"

Pup did the same.

Poor Hound was tired

of playing this game.

Hound ran to the corn maze

as fast as he could.

If that didn't work,

then nothing would!

Ah! Alone at last.

"Arf!" Not so fast!

Humph! Hound stomped
off to a stream.

He crossed the log —

a high balance beam.

Of course, that pup followed.

Go back, silly dog!

Pup's legs were wobbly,

and so was the log.

Whoopsy! Pup slipped!

He fell — *ker-PLUNK!*

Hound woofed when he saw

poor Pup get dunked.

Hound leaped in
and pulled Pup out.

He licked poor Pup

on his soft, wet snout.

Pup licked his wet fur.

And Hound did, too.

Then Pup smelled dinner.

And Hound did, too.

Pup trotted home.

Time for some chow.

Guess who followed?

Hound's the copycat now!